I0625688

Easter at Glosser's

By Robert Jeschonek

Pie Press

FIRST PIE PRESS EDITION, MARCH 2015

www.piepresspublishing.com

The text was set in Myriad Pro and Garamond.
Book design by Robert Jeschonek

ISBN-10: 0996248005
ISBN-13: 978-0-9962480-0-6

DEDICATION

To Fred, Izzy, Paul, Bill, and all the Glossers,
who've kept the magic alive after all this time.

Glosser Bros. is giving away rabbits for Easter...

"He's all yours, son." Mr. Strump grinned as he walked over with the snowball-white rabbit from the cage on the floor of the boys' clothing department. "Any Glosser Brothers customer who buys a boys' suit at Easter time gets one of these at no additional cost. Though I have to say, you've gotten an exceptional value with this one." He winked as he handed the rabbit over to Owen. "He's an actual direct descendant of Peter Cottontail himself, I'm told."

"Really?" A shiver of delight tickled the back of Owen's neck as he took the bunny from Mr. Strump. The rabbit's white fur was softer and fluffier than anything he'd ever touched in his life. "He's related to Peter?"

Mr. Strump shrugged. "That's what I was told."

"Wow." Owen held the rabbit up by its shoulders and gazed at its white-furred face. Its pink nose twitched constantly, and its long ears stood up straight. Its eyes were like glossy black marbles, staring directly at Owen.

"You're a lucky boy," said Mr. Strump. "True Cottontail rabbits are hard to come by."

Owen pulled the rabbit against his side and cradled him in his left arm as Mr. Strump had done. He could feel the rabbit's little heart fluttering wildly inside its warm, fluffy body, like the wings of a hummingbird...and that gave him an idea. "I think I'll call him Flutter."

From that moment on, Owen's life would never be the same.

"Sorry, no autographs." The old man shook his head sadly. "I don't do that sort of thing anymore."

"C'mon, please?" The twentysomething woman who'd asked for the autograph pressed a pen and folded-up white envelope at the old man. "I've loved your work since I was a kid, Mr. Talisman. And I'm only in Johnstown for the day."

Owen Talisman, a tall man in a long black overcoat and black fedora hat, shook his head again, keeping his hands stuffed in his coat pockets. "I'm sorry." Then he kept walking up Somerset Street along the Stonycreek River.

The young man who'd been walking with him--his 17-year-old great-grandson, Ethan--shrugged apologetically at the autograph seeker. "Sorry."

"No worries." The autograph seeker smiled and gave her long blonde hair a toss. "I'm just glad I finally got to

1

meet Owen Talisman in the flesh."

Ethan smiled back, charming as ever with his curly brown hair, brown eyes, and dimples. Then, he turned and jogged to catch up with his 89-year-old great-grandfather.

Some things never changed. People of all ages still loved Owen Talisman's books, especially the Bunnyburg series. They still recognized him from his photos on the books' covers and approached him on the street (or in the grocery store or doctor's office or bank) in search of autographs.

But other things did change. Owen never gave out those autographs anymore, not since that fateful day three and a half months ago. Not since Christmas, when he'd lost his partner, the illustrator of his books.

The woman who had also been his wife.

"She isn't following us, is she?" Owen didn't look back or stop walking up the sidewalk when he asked the question.

"Nope." Ethan fell in step beside him. "She's gone, Pap." That was what he'd called Owen as far back as he could remember--just "Pap," because it was easier than "Great-Grandfather" or "Great-Grandpa."

Owen had a nickname for Ethan, too: Chip, as in "chip off the old block." He said it was because Ethan reminded him of himself as a boy, especially because Ethan was the first family member who seemed to share Owen's writing talent and interest. Owen liked to say he saw that special "spark" in Ethan, the same one that had given Owen such a long and successful writing career.

Though it was true, Owen hadn't said anything like that in quite a while. Losing his wife, Melinda, had taken his own special spark right out of him.

"I just want to be left alone." Owen looked over at Ethan with a scowl. "I shouldn't have let you drag me out today."

"It's Easter, Pap," said Ethan. "You had to get to church, didn't you?"

"Is that so?" Owen stopped and leaned on a waist-high brick wall along the sidewalk, meant to keep people from falling in the Stonycreek River below. "Then tell me." He gestured at the clustered buildings of downtown Johnstown on the other side of the river. "If church is over there, why the hell are we over here?"

Ethan had a very good explanation, an excellent reason for parking on the other side of the river from church...but he wasn't about to tell Owen. Not yet, anyway. "I thought you could use a little exercise and some fresh air," he lied.

"What're you? My keeper?" Owen's scowl deepened. "I've got a 17-year-old babysitter now?"

Ethan kept his cool and shook his head. "Just a 17-year-old great-grandson. A 17-year-old friend."

Owen brushed a hand through the air in dismissal.

"This is your father's doing, isn't it? He put you up to this."

"Nope." Ethan leaned on the wall beside Owen and looked down at the river. The water was brown as mud, rushing from the heavy March rains they'd been having... glittering in the light of the first sunny day in two full weeks. "Just me, Pap. It's all good."

"Good?" Owen snorted. "Nothing's good anymore."

Ethan looked at Owen, then followed his gaze back to the river. The current swept between sloping gray concrete walls that formed a flat-bottomed "V." Erected after the flood of 1936, the walls were meant to prevent overflows in the flood-prone city. Their effectiveness was questionable, though; they hadn't seemed to do much good during the last flood in 1977.

"Enough of this." Owen pushed away from the wall. "I'm tired. Take me home."

Ethan felt a shot of panic in his belly. "We haven't gone to church yet," he said, though church wasn't what he was worried about.

"I don't care." Owen stuffed his hands back in his overcoat pockets. "I just want to go home."

Ethan's heart pounded. He had a secret plan, and taking Owen home wasn't part of it. He had to get him to a certain place at a certain time; the place was just a few blocks away, and the time was fifteen minutes from now.

Without arousing Owen's suspicions, he had to keep him downtown for another fifteen minutes.

Thinking it over, Ethan came up with the perfect delaying tactic, one that tied right in with the reason they were there in the first place. "Tell me the story, Pap," he said.

Owen frowned. "What story?"

"You know," said Ethan. "The one about Easter at Glosser Bros."

"Forget it." Owen glared across the river, in the direction not only of downtown Johnstown but Glosser Bros. Department Store. At least it had been Glosser's Department Store until 25 years ago, when it had closed its doors for good.

"Then I'll tell it," said Ethan. "I've heard it so many times, I think I know it by heart anyway."

Owen sighed. "I'm walking back to the car."

"Be my guest." Ethan shrugged. "But you'll have a long wait while I finish the story, since I have the keys."

Owen slumped, looking disgusted. But he didn't storm off to the car and leave Ethan standing there alone.

"Good." Ethan cleared his throat. "It all started three days before Easter in 1935..."

*****

Eight-year-old Owen Talisman had to fight his way through the crowd to get a look at the day's main attraction on the first floor of the Glosser Bros. Department Store. It seemed like every kid in the place--and every parent, too--was mobbing the area near the base of the stairway to the second floor and the top of the stairs leading to the grocery department in the basement.

They all wanted to get closer to the incubator, just like Owen.

Though Owen was small for his age and on the scrawny side, he wasn't about to give up. He pushed and twisted his way through the mob, drawn by the siren song emanating from the incubator...the irresistible chirping of hundreds of tiny creatures.

Grunting, Owen struggled to squeeze between a tubby girl and a stocky boy, the last obstacles separating him from his goal. He finally made it through, and the spectacle unveiled before him.

The incubator was four feet wide on each side and six feet high. It had four levels, each filled with a rainbow of multicolored chicks, their downy feathers dyed pink or blue or green or left a natural bright yellow.

Each level had an open front section where the chicks hopped around, eating and drinking from little metal troughs. Each of these front sections had a metal screen around it to keep the chicks from getting out while still letting Glosser's shoppers watch their antics.

The rear section of each level was enclosed with metal walls, floors, and ceilings. These boxed-in rear sections provided a refuge where the chicks could rest away from prying eyes, staying warm in the glow of heating bulbs mounted in the ceiling.

Front to back, top to bottom, the incubator was something to see...especially set up in the middle of the Glosser Bros. Department Store like that. Shoppers-- adults as much as children--couldn't seem to get enough of watching the colorful chicks frolic while money changed hands and the smell of roasting nuts (a Glosser's trademark) wafted around them.

As for Owen, he had seen it before, in previous Easter seasons, but he never tired of it. His family had a few chickens; sometimes, there were peeps in the coop. But only at Glosser's at Easter time did he see this many peeps at once, all bouncing and chirping--a small army of adorable baby birds, crying out to be picked up and played with.

And that was exactly what he was going to do before leaving Glosser's and taking the streetcar back to Moxham Borough that day. One of those peeps would be his, no matter what happened.

Mesmerized, he reached toward the incubator, intending

to press a fingertip against the screen and see if any of the chicks responded. Then, suddenly, a hand grabbed hold of his left upper arm. He resisted, hoping the hand would let him go...but it didn't.

Instead, it jerked him back out of the crowd and spun him around. Just like that, he stood facing his mother, who didn't look happy at all. "Owen Talisman! Who do you think you are, running off like that?"

"But the peeps!" Owen threw back his free arm and pointed at the incubator. "What if they run out before we get one?"

"Then we'll just have to run after them, I suppose." Owen's mother was making a joke. Her dark eyes twinkled when she said it.

"No!" Owen's face wrinkled with anger. "I mean what if they give them all away?"

"Don't worry, honey." Mom smiled reassuringly. "They have plenty to go around."

With that, she turned and headed for the elevators in the middle of the store, pulling Owen along after her. In spite of what she'd said, he couldn't help looking back over his shoulder at the crowd around the incubator.

It was a Glosser Bros. tradition, giving away a peep to every child who entered the store at Easter time with a parent. And it was true, they had always had enough that

Owen had never left empty-handed.

But still...who could say they wouldn't run out this year? Especially by the time Owen got done with his trip to the second floor and the major project that always seemed to him to take an eternity.

Though it was true, another wonderful prize awaited if he could just get through it. All he had to do was survive the torture without cracking...which he knew from experience would be no mean feat.

Just thinking about it made him gulp as he reluctantly stepped into the right-hand elevator car with Mom. As the doors closed, he even considered bolting and making a run for it.

But to get the reward, he knew he would have to tough it out, no matter how terrible it would be.

"What floor please?" asked the elevator operator, a pleasant, dark-skinned woman who knew Owen by name.

"Two, please." Mom smiled and patted Owen's head.

"Let me guess." The elevator operator raised an eyebrow at Owen. "Time for some new clothes, child?"

"Special clothes," said Mom. "We have to get him ready for Easter."

"Time for a new suit?" The elevator operator pulled the lever on the wall beside her, and the car climbed upward. "A new church suit?"

"And shoes," said Mom. "Isn't that right, Owen?"

"Yes, ma'am." Owen's voice was full of despair. "That's right."

The women laughed, and the elevator car stopped moving. Owen shivered with dread.

"Second floor." As the outer gate slid open, the elevator operator pulled the inner gate open, too. "Boys' suits and shoes. I hope you find some nice ones, Owen."

"Thanks." Owen didn't sound especially grateful.

The elevator operator leaned down and whispered confidentially. "Don't forget to ask about the giveaway, honey. One free bunny rabbit with every new suit."

Owen's frown became a small smile. It was exactly the reward he'd been anticipating.

*****

"Here." The salesman, a man in his late twenties or early thirties with dark hair, tugged a navy blue suit coat off a hanger and handed it to Owen. "Give this one a try."

Owen pulled the coat on quickly, without worrying about how it hung. His goal was to get done as fast as possible, so he could get to the prize at the end, then get his peep from the incubator downstairs and go home.

To say he hated trying on clothes would be the

understatement of the decade. He'd only tried on three suit coats so far, but he felt like he'd tried on three dozen.

"Hmm." Mom leaned back and stared at him with narrowed eyes, tapping her bottom lip with a fingertip. "I don't like the cut of that one, do you?"

The salesman, whose name was Mr. Strump, straightened the coat on Owen's shoulders. "It's one of our top sellers." He stepped around Owen and fixed his lapels, which were folded inside the breast of the coat. Then, he stepped back beside Mom and joined her in staring. "Turn around, young man. Slowly, if you please."

As Owen turned in a slow circle, his eyes went straight to the big metal cage on the floor in the middle of the boys' department. Other children milled around it, gaping at what was inside and poking fingers through the bars, eager to touch and play with the occupants.

As for the rabbits inside the cage, they just huddled together and nibbled lettuce and bits of carrot. Owen's heart beat fast as he watched and wondered which animal he would get to take home as his very own personal Easter bunny.

"I don't think so." Mr. Strump helped him out of the navy blue coat and draped it over its hanger. "Let's try another. Something in brown, perhaps?"

Another. Owen winced, fighting the impulse to stomp his foot in anger. He hated the thought of trying on one more coat, but he hated the thought of not getting a free bunny even more.

Mom walked around a circular rack, running her hand along the suits hanging there. "Wait." Her hand stopped, and she pulled a light brown suit off the rack. "What about this one?"

Owen clenched his teeth as Mr. Strump reached for the suit. But then, when he put on the coat, a funny thing happened.

He didn't hate it.

It fit him perfectly. When he walked over to have a look in the mirror on the wall, he liked what he saw.

Mom seemed to be right in tune with him. "There we go." She sounded pleased. "Very nice."

"Good, good," said Mr. Strump.

Without being told, Owen turned slowly to look at the back and sides of the coat in the mirror. He was happy, because he'd found the right suit coat at last...and because now he could get to the good part.

Or so he thought.

"Now let's try on the pants as well." Mr. Strump held out the hanger with the matching trousers folded over the cross bar.

As much as he liked the suit, Owen still slumped as he took the pants and headed into the dressing room. Was he ever going to get that bunny?

*****

Luckily, the pants fit fine. So did the first pair of brown dress shoes that Owen tried on with them.

Mr. Strump wrote up a sales slip for the purchases--including a dark brown tie that Mom had picked out--then walked it over to the cashier's desk for the boys' department. The young woman working there had short, dark hair, brown eyes, and a pretty smile. She took the slip from Mr. Strump, told Mom how much she owed, then waited as Mom counted out the money from her pocketbook.

Mom had enough money to buy new clothes for Owen now that his father was back to work at Bethlehem Steel. Things had been tough for a few months before that, when Dad had been laid off...but things were better now. Mom had even paid back the credit she'd gotten from Glosser's, the "Glosser bucks" scrip vouchers that had helped her buy groceries during the layoff.

So Owen would have a new outfit for Easter that year... and a new rabbit, of course, which was something he wanted much more.

The cashier put the money and sales slip in a metal capsule about a foot long. Turning, she opened a door in the metal tube behind her, which ran straight up to the ceiling. She placed the capsule in the tube, then shut the door and pressed a button on the wall. The tube made a whooshing sound, and the capsule shot away through the store.

It was all part of what they called a pneumatic tube system, which used air pressure to transport sales slips and cash to the money office on the fourth floor and back again. Owen always loved to see it in action; once, a salesperson had even arranged for him to visit the money office and watch firsthand as the capsules flew up from the lower floors, then were cracked open, fed the correct change, and sent back down again.

This time, it took only a few minutes for the capsule to return to the cashier's desk. As she waited, the cashier packed Owen's new shoes in a box, then wrapped the suit in a paper sleeve with a hole at the top that fit over the hooked tip of the suit's wire hanger.

She had just finished packaging the purchases when the capsule whooshed back into the tube. "Here we are," she said, opening the tube and capsule and pulling out a receipt and change.

The cashier counted the change into Mom's hand, gave her the receipt, and thanked her for shopping at Glosser's.

"Thank you." Mom smiled and turned to go. "Happy Easter to you, too."

At which point, Owen started to panic. Heart hammering in his chest, he looked at Mom, then at the rabbit cage, wondering what he should do next.

They couldn't just walk out of there without the most important thing, could they?

"Oh, wait." Mom turned back to the cashier. "What about our complimentary rabbit?"

"Don't worry." Mr. Strump zipped past on his way to the bunny cage. "I wasn't going to let you forget that." He shot Owen a knowing wink.

And Owen's mood instantly shifted from worry to excitement.

With his back to Owen and Mom, Mr. Strump opened a door atop the cage and lifted something out. At first, Owen couldn't see what he held; then, after closing the cage door, Mr. Strump turned to face him.

"Perfect." Mr. Strump nodded and smiled at the fat white rabbit in the crook of his arm.

Owen's eyes widened. The other rabbits were brown or gray or black or white with spots and patches of other colors--but this one was pure, snowball white. He'd noticed him before, when he'd first sized up the cage; this was the only pure white rabbit of the lot.

And he was going to be Owen's personal pet.

"He's all yours, son." Mr. Strump grinned as he walked

over with the white rabbit. "Any Glosser Brothers customer who buys a boys' suit at Easter time gets one of these at no additional cost. Though I have to say, you've gotten an exceptional value with this one." He winked as he handed the rabbit over to Owen. "He's an actual direct descendant of Peter Cottontail himself, I'm told."

"Really?" A shiver of delight tickled the back of Owen's neck as he took the bunny from Mr. Strump. The rabbit's white fur was softer and fluffier than anything he'd ever touched in his life. "He's related to Peter?"

Mr. Strump shrugged. "That's what I was told."

"Wow." Owen held the rabbit up by its shoulders and gazed at its white-furred face. Its pink nose twitched constantly, and its long ears stood up straight. Its eyes were like glossy black marbles, staring directly at Owen.

"You're a lucky boy," said Mr. Strump. "True Cottontail rabbits are hard to come by."

"They are?" said Owen.

"Oh, yes," said Mr. Strump. "You'll have to take extra good care of him, so someday he can take Peter's place on the bunny trail."

Owen looked up at him in alarm. "Someday when?"

"Many years from now," said Mom. "Don't worry, you'll have lots of time together before then."

"Good." Owen pulled the rabbit against his side and

cradled him in his left arm as Mr. Strump had done. He could feel the rabbit's little heart fluttering wildly inside its warm, fluffy body, like the wings of a hummingbird...and that gave him an idea. "I think I'll call him Flutter."

"Fine by me." Mr. Strump winked. "I'll let the Bunny Brotherhood know as soon as you leave."

Owen gaped at him. There was a Bunny Brotherhood?

"Thank you so much, Mr. Strump." Mom waved and nudged Owen in the direction of the elevator. "We always love coming to Glosser's at Easter."

"Where else could you find the one-and-only Flutter Cottontail?" asked Mr. Strump. "And those adorable peeps, of course."

"The peeps!" Owen's head shot up from staring at the rabbit. "We need to get our peep!"

"We will, honey." The paper sleeve over the suit crumpled as Mom draped it over her arm.

"We need to hurry!" The rabbit bounced in Owen's arms as he ran toward the elevator doors in the middle of the second floor.

"No, you need to slow down!" shouted Mom. "You'll get your free peep, Owen...won't he, Mr. Strump?"

"Of course you'll get your peep," said Mr. Strump. "Cottontail rabbits are magic, aren't they?"

Owen stopped running and grinned down at Flutter. As

a descendant of Peter Cottontail himself, he had to be magic.

"Cottontails make good things happen," said Mr. Strump. "They'll change your life for the better, son. Believe it!"

*****

Bunnyburg. That was what the sign said, the one that Owen's dad had carved with his woodworking tools. It was the name of Flutter Cottontail's new home.

It was also the last piece of that home, a hutch that Dad had built in the back yard of the family's house in Moxham Borough with a little help from Owen. Dad even let Owen hammer in the last nail to fix the sign in place over the door of the hutch. Then, the two of them stood back and admired their handiwork.

The sturdy wood frame formed a box that was open to the air on all sides. Flutter wouldn't be able to get out, though; chicken wire lined every opening.

"What do you say, Owen?" asked Dad. "Will it do the trick?"

Owen grinned and nodded. "He'll love it, Dad."

"Did we put in enough straw, do you think?"

Owen cocked his head to one side and tapped his lower lip with a fingertip. "Maybe just a little more, Dad."

They added more straw in the bottom of the hutch, spreading it around and patting it down. Then, Owen fetched Flutter from the deep cardboard box where he'd been living for the past two days since his arrival from Glosser's.

"Home sweet home, Flutter Cottontail," said Owen as he lifted the white rabbit through the open door of the hutch. "Welcome to Bunnyburg."

Once Flutter was inside, Owen placed a little dish of water in the corner closest to the door. Dad put in a handful of bright green lettuce, and Flutter started nibbling on it right away.

"He looks pretty comfy in there." Dad tipped back his brown fedora and folded his arms across his chest. "Looks like a happy rabbit, if you ask me."

Owen reached in and stroked Flutter's soft fur. "Blondie's happy, too, Dad." He was talking about the peep from Glosser's; he'd named her Blondie. She had her own box full of straw in the chicken coop, and he played with her often, though not as often as he played with Flutter. He loved both animals, but Flutter was more special to him...maybe because he was a direct descendant of Peter Cottontail and all.

"I'm proud of you, son." Dad reached down and tousled Owen's hair. "Being kind to animals is the mark of a good person."

Owen felt a surge of happiness...but then something

he'd been worrying about came up over him. "Do you think the Bunny Brotherhood will ever take him away?" he asked.

"The Bunny Brotherhood?"

"Yeah," said Owen. "Mr. Strump said there's a Bunny Brotherhood. And he said Flutter will have to take Peter's place on the bunny trail someday. What if the Bunny Brotherhood takes him away to take Peter's place?"

Dad narrowed his eyes thoughtfully. "I don't think that will happen, as long as you take good enough care of him. Keep him happy enough that he'll never want to leave."

"You really think that'll work?"

Dad nodded. "It worked for me. Why do you think I never hopped away from this place?"

Owen shrugged. "Because you're happy?"

"That's right," said Dad. "You and your mother always keep me so happy, I never want to leave." With a smile, he rapped on the frame of the hutch. "Just do the same for Flutter here, and things ought to work out just fine."

*****

But things didn't work out so fine after all.

On a sunny May morning two weeks after Easter, Owen walked out to feed and water Flutter. When he saw the open door of the hutch, he dropped the lettuce and dish of water on the ground and cried out in alarm.

Running to the hutch, he saw that Flutter was gone. All that remained were some tufts of white fur and little round pellets of poop in the mashed-down straw.

The rabbit had disappeared, but Owen grabbed the hutch and shook it anyway. Nothing moved inside except the rattling straw and pellets.

Just then, Mom ran out of the house behind him. "What happened? What's going on?"

Tears streamed down Owen's face as he dropped the hutch on its wooden stand. "Flutter's gone!"

Mom looked around. "Maybe he just got out. Are you sure you didn't leave the door unlatched?"

"I'm sure of it! I never leave it unlatched!"

"All right." Mom clapped her hands together. "So however he got out, he might be somewhere nearby. Let's start searching."

"But what if it was the Bunny Brotherhood? What if they came and took him to take the place of Peter?"

"Let's hope for the best." Mom gestured at the left side of the yard. "You look that way, and I'll look over here." She gestured at the right side of the yard. "Maybe he'll turn up."

But he never turned up. The fluffy white rabbit would have been tough to miss among the greens in the vegetable garden or the berry bushes and weeds around the edge of the yard...but Mom and Owen never caught a glimpse of him.

Neither did Dad, when he got home from work that afternoon and joined the search. Neither did any of the neighbors, when Dad asked them to look around for a trace of the rabbit.

Flutter Cottontail was gone for good.

*****

Mrs. Malonek next door had a theory about the disappearance. She thought that someone had taken Flutter, all right...but not the Bunny Brotherhood. It was the Great Depression, after all, and times were tough; she wouldn't put it past someone, she said, to have stolen Flutter for the cookpot.

As true as that might have been, it wasn't something Owen needed to hear. It made him all the more downcast in days to come, as his parents gave up searching, and the reality of life without Flutter set in.

All he could think about, day and night, was the missing rabbit. He slogged through school, barely able to focus on a word the teacher was saying. He walked home in a daze, not stopping to play stickball or marbles or cowboys and Indians with his friends. And when he got home, he went straight to his room and moped, lying on his bed and staring up at the ceiling.

He was miserable.

"Why don't you go play with Blondie?" asked Mom, trying to take his mind off Flutter. "She's probably starting to feel lonely, don't you think?"

"I don't care," said Owen. "I want Flutter back."

"Honey." Mom sat beside him on the bed. "I'm sorry, but I don't think he's coming back. I think you're going to have to let him go."

"I won't. I can't." With that, Owen rolled over, turning his back to her. "I miss him too much."

"Don't worry," said Mom. "This too shall pass."

"No it won't," said Owen. "It'll never pass."

"It will," Mom said reassuringly. "You'll see. Somehow, things will get better."

Owen didn't believe her. In the days that followed, he just felt worse and worse. He couldn't imagine ever feeling better again in his life, no matter what happened.

Not unless Flutter came back to him.

*****

A month after Easter, Owen was still depressed about

Flutter. His parents were more worried about him than ever, but nothing they tried could snap him out of his despair.

He just couldn't accept that Flutter was gone. Whether the rabbit had been stolen and eaten or taken away to replace Peter Cottontail, Owen couldn't seem to move on without him.

Then, one Saturday morning, there was a loud knock at the front door. A moment later, Mom called for Owen, who was reading a book in his bedroom.

Reluctantly, Owen put the book down and walked to the parlor. When he got there, he saw that Mom was standing in the doorway, holding the front screen door open. She was looking down at a little brown basket on the porch floorboards outside.

"What is it?" asked Owen.

"You tell me." Mom nodded at the basket. "It has your name in it."

Frowning, Owen stepped out for a closer look. Inside the basket was a folded piece of white paper with two words printed on it: OWEN TALISMAN.

There was something else in the basket, too. When Owen bent down and pulled out the folded paper, he saw a tiny tuft of white fur stuck underneath it.

White fur. Suddenly, his heart started pounding.

"Is that what I think it is?" asked Mom.

Owen didn't answer. Instead, he unfolded the paper and read the note that was printed inside.

He couldn't keep his hands from shaking with excitement. He read the note three times before Mom insisted he read it aloud to her.

"'Special message arriving tonight. Meet at the big apple tree on the edge of the woods at the top of the hill at sunset.'"

"Wow," said Mom. "What do you think that's about?"

Owen couldn't take his eyes off the paper. He just kept staring at the words...and what was below them, on the bottom half of the page.

"Are you going to the apple tree tonight?" Mom's eyes were wide, and she was smiling. "Are you going to find out what the special message is?"

"I guess I'd better." Owen pointed at the marks on the bottom of the page. They looked like a bunny's paw print, stamped in ink. "He signed it. I think Flutter signed it."

*****

It was after eight o'clock when Owen and Dad set out for the woods. The sun was lowering in the sky, slowly drifting toward the rooftops of the neighborhood.

The air was cool and smelled of sweet spring blossoms

and new-mown grass. The laughter of children and the barking of dogs abounded, though the end of daylight and playtime was fast approaching. Lamps flicked on in windows, one by one, lighting up parlors and dining rooms from within for passersby to see in bright relief against the coming of night's darkness.

All these details made stronger impressions than usual on Owen's young mind. Normally, they were background noise, part of his everyday world...but tonight, they were part of something infinitely more thrilling. He was on his way to a secret meeting, one that might bring him face to face with something magical and extraordinary. In the course of this meeting, he would receive some kind of "special message" that might provide the answer to the biggest mystery of his life so far.

Namely, what had become of Flutter Cottontail?

"Are you nervous?" asked Dad as they turned the corner from Linden Avenue onto Bond Street and headed up the hill.

"A little," said Owen. "What do you think the special message will be?"

"Who knows?" Dad was holding Owen's hand and gave it a squeeze. "I guess we'll find out soon enough."

Near the top of the hill, Owen stopped, and Dad stopped with him. From where they stood, Owen could see the big old apple tree at the edge of the woods.

Squinting, he looked for some sign of whomever he was going to meet. Mostly, he looked for a glimpse of Flutter's white fur, because that was what he secretly expected to see.

But there wasn't any white fur in sight. Around the base of the apple tree, Owen saw nothing but shadows.

"This is it." Dad gave Owen's hand a shake. "So do you want me to go with you the rest of the way?"

Owen swallowed hard and pulled his hand free of Dad's. He was getting more nervous as the big moment approached, but he was determined to act like a big boy. "I'll go myself."

"Good luck then," said Dad. "I'll be right here if you need me."

Owen had twenty feet to go to get to the apple tree. Halfway there, he stopped, frozen in place with fearful shivering.

Then, he heard footsteps behind him. He felt a familiar hand on his shoulder and instantly felt at ease.

It was Dad, of course. "Can I come with you after all?" he asked. "I can't wait to see who shows up and find out what the message is."

Owen nodded, and they continued on together.

When they finally reached the tree, Owen heard a rustling noise that made him jump. Instinctively, he grabbed Dad's hand and held it tight.

"Hello?" said Dad. "Who's there?"

Owen heard more rustling from the brush around the tree. Then, suddenly, a figure emerged from behind the broad trunk.

Owen felt a pang of disappointment, because the figure was human. He'd been hoping for Flutter Cottontail, but instead, he saw a man looking back at him from the shadows.

"Greetings." The man was old, with a full gray beard and a big, round face. He wore ragged, mismatched clothes: a rumpled top hat, a tattered blue jacket, a gray work shirt, and faded jeans. The hodge-podge outfit put Owen in mind of the hobos he saw passing through town, the ones who sometimes went to Glosser's and were given a free meal by the Glosser family to sustain them. "Are you Owen Talisman?" The man's voice was deep and gravelly.

"Y-yes." Owen nodded. The man had made no hostile moves, but Owen was still glad that Dad had come with him.

"Very good." The man tipped his hat and smiled. "My name is Lightfoot. Flutter Cottontail sent me."

"He did?" Owen's eyes grew wide as softballs.

Lightfoot reached into a pocket of his jacket and pulled out a tuft of white fur, which he handed to Owen. "Indeed he did."

Owen marveled at the tuft and showed it to Dad, who grinned and nodded.

"Very good to meet you." Lightfoot reached out and shook Owen's hand, then cast a suspicious look in Dad's direction. "And I suppose you can vouch for him?"

Owen nodded. "That's my Dad. He's okay."

"All right then." Lightfoot shook Dad's hand. "Now let's get down to business. I have a special message from Flutter." Opening his jacket wide, he pointed at a badge pinned to the left chest of his work shirt. The badge was silver and simply designed, with the letters "BB" printed in white in the middle of it. "Y'see, I'm a representative of the Bunny Brotherhood."

"Really?" said Owen.

"Absolutely." Lightfoot stuck up the index and middle fingers of his right hand and wiggled them back and forth like rabbit ears. "There's the high sign for you, Owen. Any time you see it, you'll know for sure it's one of us."

Owen nodded slowly.

Lightfoot ended the salute and lowered his hand. "Flutter sends his apologies. He wished he could make it himself, but he's just too busy. It isn't easy stepping into the shoes of Peter Cottontail, the most famous rabbit who ever lived."

"Flutter's okay?" asked Owen. "He didn't get thrown in a cookpot and eaten?"

Lightfoot laughed. "Of course not! He's just fine! He's

a magical Cottontail, isn't he?"

Owen felt a deep relief at hearing the news. The shadow that had been hanging over him for weeks suddenly lifted.

"Flutter's better than ever, actually," said Lightfoot. "He's the new king of Bunnyburg, and he's really making the place shine."

"Is he ever coming back?" asked Owen.

Lightfoot squinted his left eye and shook his head. "I doubt it," he said. "I mean, he might pass through on Easter morning, but he'll be too busy to stop off and chew the fat with you. Understand?"

"Well, can I go and visit him in Bunnyburg, then?" asked Owen.

Lightfoot met Dad's gaze, then cleared his throat. "Sorry, but no. No humans allowed. Not even the Bunny Brotherhood."

"But that's not fair!" Owen felt the pressure of tears building up in his eyes, getting ready to burst forth. "I miss him so much."

"Which is exactly why I'm here." Lightfoot raised his hand and wiggled his two fingers again. "To report the latest news so you'll know exactly what's going on in Flutter's life. He said that's the least we could do, after you took care of him so well."

Owen swallowed hard, holding back tears.

"There's just one catch, Owen," said Lightfoot. "I need you to do one thing before I tell you the latest."

"What's that?" asked Owen.

"What I'm about to tell you is confidential information," said Lightfoot. "It can only be shared with trusted members of the Bunny Brotherhood."

Owen frowned. "But I'm not..."

"Which is why you need to join the Bunny Brotherhood before I tell you a single thing. You, too, big guy." Lightfoot wiggled his two fingers at Dad.

Dad shrugged. "Fair enough." He raised a hand and wiggled his fingers just like Lightfoot.

Owen did the same.

"Very good." Lightfoot grinned, revealing several gaps in his smile where teeth were missing. "Now repeat after me. In the name of the great carrot patch, I hereby swear to uphold the code of the Bunny Brotherhood."

Owen and Dad repeated the oath word-for-word.

"I swear always to help rabbits whenever I can," continued Lightfoot. "Setting out carrots and lettuce to feed them...keeping the bunny trails and burrows clear for them... chasing away the cats and dogs who hunt them...and doing everything in my power to keep all bunnies safe from harm."

Owen and Dad finished the oath, and everyone wiggled their fingers in the salute that Lightfoot had taught them.

When Lightfoot wiggled his nose like a bunny, they did that, too.

"Congratulations," said Lightfoot. "You are now official members of the Bunny Brotherhood...and I may now tell you the story of Flutter Cottontail's adventures since returning to the magical land of Bunnyburg."

With that, he began to tell Flutter's story. Dad listened with interest, leaning a shoulder against the trunk of the apple tree.

And Owen hung on every word with attention so rapt, nothing could tear him away until the last word of the story had been spoken.

*****

Later, Owen walked back down the hill of Bond Street with Dad, talking about the amazing visit they'd had with Lightfoot. The messenger of the Bunny Brotherhood had told them so many wonderful things before he'd gone, all about Flutter and the kingdom of Bunnyburg.

Then, at the end, he'd told them the most wonderful thing of all. It was all Owen could think about, in fact.

"I regret to say I must go now," Lightfoot had said. "But have no fear. This won't be the last you hear of Flutter Cottontail."

"What do you mean?" Owen had asked breathlessly.

"I mean Flutter isn't going to leave you in the dark." Lightfoot had shaken his head slowly, emphatically. "From time to time, he will send a fellow member of the Bunny Brotherhood to bring you the latest news report from Bunnyburg. You'll be notified of the time and meeting place just as you were today."

"When?" Owen had shouted, unable to contain his excitement. "When will I get the next report?"

"It depends," Lightfoot had told him. "You'll just have to wait and see."

"But I'll definitely get another report?"

"Now that you're part of the Brotherhood, you have to get one." Lightfoot had nodded and taken off his "BB" badge. "It's one of your rights and privileges."

Then, Lightfoot had pinned the badge to Owen's shirt and tousled his hair. Moments later, with one last wiggling fingers salute, he'd disappeared into the darkness of the woods as if he'd never been at the apple tree in the first place.

Now, on the way home with Dad, Owen couldn't stop looking at and touching the badge on his chest. And he couldn't stop thinking about the next news report from Bunnyburg.

"When do you think it will be?" he asked Dad. "When will I get the next message?"

Dad shrugged. "We'll have to wait and see, like Lightfoot said."

"But I can't wait," said Owen.

Dad chuckled. "Sure you can. After tonight's news report, you'll have plenty to keep you busy until then."

Owen frowned up at him. "What do you mean?"

"Don't you think you'd better write down the news you heard?" said Dad. "Somebody has to put the stories down on paper, for posterity's sake."

"Posterity?" Owen scowled at the word.

"History," said Dad. "You need to save the stories for future generations. Maybe even draw some pictures to go with them. Think you're up to the job?"

"Yeah!" Owen kicked a stone down the hill victoriously.

"It's a lot of responsibility," Dad said sternly. "Are you sure you can do it?"

"Yeah, Dad! I can do a great job at it!"

"Okay then." Dad smiled and patted his head.

"I'll start tonight, as soon as we get home!" said Owen.

"Isn't it already past your bedtime?"

"But I don't want to forget anything," said Owen.

"Maybe you can do a little, then," said Dad. "Just until you fall asleep."

"I won't fall asleep. I'll work all night and get all the stories and pictures on paper."

"Sounds good." Dad didn't seem too worried that Owen would manage to stay up all night. "I can't wait to see what you come up with."

"Do you think I can send a copy to Flutter Cottontail?" asked Owen.

"I don't see why not," said Dad. "Who knows? Other folks might want to read it, too."

"You think so?"

Dad grinned and reached for Owen's hand. "You never know."

*****

Lightfoot's promise came true. One month after his visit, another note showed up in a basket on Owen's front porch, inviting him to return to the apple tree for another special message.

This time, a different man showed up, a young man with black hair and glasses. Like Lightfoot, he wore mismatched hobo-style clothes...and a top hat and Bunny Brotherhood badge. He said his name was Fencedigger, and he told stories of Flutter's adventures that were even more amazing than the stories Lightfoot had told.

A month after that, another invitation arrived, and another top-hatted representative of the Bunny Brotherhood arrived--this one an elderly woman with silver hair and bright green eyes. She nibbled a carrot the whole time she spoke and gave Owen a piece of hard candy when her stories were done.

More Bunny Brotherhood messengers came to see Owen in the months that followed. And Owen faithfully wrote down and drew every story they told him.

He kept everything that he wrote and drew in notebooks under his bed--a detailed record of events in Bunnyburg and the epic life and times of its king, Flutter Cottontail. Owen made copies that he gave to the Bunny Brotherhood messengers to give to Flutter...but he always kept the originals safe at home.

And over time, he added stories to them that he hadn't heard from the Brotherhood, stories that he had made up on his own. He had to, because he needed new stories, and the Brotherhood came less and less often over time; around Christmas, they stopped coming altogether, only reappearing at Easter time the next year.

By then, Owen had filled entire notebooks with new stories. He was much more interested in creating his own Bunnyburg stories than hearing the ones that the Brotherhood messengers told him at the apple tree.

And when he finally found out, as an adult, that the messengers had all been hobos after all, recruited and paid by Dad to help him get over Flutter's disappearance, it didn't trouble him at all. Because Owen recognized that Dad had kept the magic alive for him. He realized that those emissaries of Flutter Cottontail had given him hope and wonder and a gift that could change the direction of his life.

For those notebooks became the foundation of his writing career, the basis of the Bunnyburg series that would someday capture the imaginations of children around the world. It was a series that would bring him all the good things life had to offer: money, recognition, travel...and the love of a good woman who was also his artistic partner and number one supporter.

Though, ultimately, the books could not do one particular thing for him, one thing that mattered more than anything in the world.

They could not keep his wife alive when she got sick, and they could not bring her back when she died.

*****

Ethan Talisman left that last part out when he finished retelling the story on Easter morning along the bank of the Stonycreek River. Great-grandfather Owen didn't need another reminder of what had happened to the love of his life, Melinda.

Though, from the look on Owen's face, Ethan thought maybe he'd filled in that last part on his own.

"The end." Ethan smiled. "So how'd I do, Pap? Did I tell it right?"

Owen shrugged, looking grimmer than ever. "Can we finally go now?" He gestured in the general direction of Ethan's car. "I want to go home."

Ethan kept smiling. He was determined to carry out his secret plan in spite of Owen's resistance. "Right after church." Checking the watch on his wrist, he saw the storytelling had taken just long enough. There were five minutes left until he had to get Owen to where he needed to be for the surprise to occur.

"No church." Owen shook his head darkly. "Church does nothing for me anymore."

"So go through the motions. Humor me." Ethan took Owen by the arm and gestured toward the Franklin Street Bridge, which was less than half a block away and would take them to downtown proper. "Maybe I just want to have one more traditional Easter with my Pap."

A gust of wind swept up from the river, and Owen pulled the fedora tighter on his head. Otherwise, he didn't budge. His face, which once upon a time had been merry more often than not, was etched with the ingrained scowl of personal loss and endless misery.

"Please, Pap?" Ethan tugged Owen's arm. "Just this one more time?"

Owen seemed no more inclined to cooperate, and Ethan was starting to think his plan was doomed. The old man shrugged off Ethan's hand and glared at him with the same dark expression, lacking any trace of the spark he'd once had in such abundance. Owen steeled himself, expecting a nasty refusal that made his plan even less likely to succeed.

But then, without a word, Owen started walking toward the bridge.

Ethan cheered silently and fell in step beside him. As long as Owen kept moving and didn't pull a fast one of some kind, there was still time for everything to happen exactly as Ethan had planned.

A car beeped as it passed them, and Owen didn't react. Following the right turn of the sidewalk, he started across the bridge above the muddy, rushing water.

"You're more her chip than mine," said the old man.

Ethan frowned. "Huh?"

"Your great-grandmother," said Owen. "You're more like her than me. So stubborn. Always trying to get me to do the right thing." He nodded. "When I said you were a chip off the old block, I meant that you were a chip off her block more than mine."

Ethan was surprised. "Really?"

"Now you know my secret." Owen snorted. "One of them, anyway."

As they crossed the bridge together in the Easter morning sun, Ethan thought about his great-grandma, Melinda. He remembered her delicate features, her bright blue eyes, and the way she'd always tipped her head when she'd listened to what he said. Echoes of her sweet voice and girlish giggle rippled through his memory.

Owen could not have paid him a higher compliment, he decided, than saying that she was the block from which he'd been chipped the most.

"I miss her, too," said Ethan. "I miss her every day."

"Good." Owen didn't look up from the sidewalk when he said it.

A few more steps, and the bridge ended. Ethan and Owen continued past the Conrad Building, an ancient flatiron-style structure that had partially crumbled into the river.

When they got to the intersection of Franklin and Vine streets, they had to wait for a few cars to roll past. Then, the light changed, and the pedestrian signal on the opposite corner flashed the white outline of a walking man for their benefit.

The two of them proceeded down Franklin, then stopped for another light at the intersection with Main

Street. At that point, Ethan couldn't help looking toward Central Park, where his plan would reach its culmination. He couldn't see anything out of the ordinary from where he was standing, which was good; he didn't want anything to tip off Owen before the time was right.

"I expect you to take me home the instant church is over," said Owen as they crossed Main. "No brunch nonsense and no unexpected stops or drives through the countryside. Capische?"

"Got it." Ethan slowed his pace fractionally, glancing across the street at Central Park. There was no way to know if everything was ready; he would just have to trust that his helpers had all done their jobs.

For his part, Owen seemed to have no inkling that anything unusual was in the wind. "Let's get this over with," he said, sparing not a single glance at the park as he stalked along the sidewalk.

He didn't look at the big brick building across Locust Street from the park, either, though it had once played a prominent role in his life. That building had once housed the Glosser Bros. Department Store; it looked much the same now as it had on that long-ago day in 1935 when Owen had gotten Blondie the chick and Flutter Cottontail...though the signage and awnings that had once adorned it were long gone.

Was it too painful for Owen to look at that building--now a county property full of offices and courtrooms--and remember the good times he'd once had there? Would it hurt too much to recall the experiences he'd shared at Glosser's with his loved ones, so many of whom were now gone?

It was probably best to leave those questions unspoken, Ethan thought.

Up ahead, at the end of the block, people were filing into the Franklin Street United Methodist Church. For all Owen knew, he'd be filing inside the place, too.

Then, suddenly, his immediate destiny became less predictable.

"Pap, hold on." Ethan caught Owen's elbow and stopped him from merging with the flow of churchgoers. "Look over there." He pointed at Central Park across the street, at the bench closest to the corner of Franklin and Locust.

"What?" Owen looked annoyed.

"That little girl." Ethan took a step toward the curb. "She's sitting there alone, crying."

Owen looked where Ethan was pointing, then brushed a hand through the air dismissively. "Not our business."

"You don't think?" Ethan stood a moment more, watching the little blonde girl on the bench. She was clearly sobbing; her head was bowed, her shoulders were rising and falling. "But what if you're wrong? What if she needs help?"

Owen gestured toward the crowd filing into the church. "Plenty of other people around if she does."

"Come on." Ethan waited till the street was clear of traffic, then stepped down off the curb. "It can't hurt to make sure she's okay."

"Go ahead," said Owen. "I'll meet you inside." He turned to head for the entrance of the church.

At which point, Ethan hopped back up onto the curb and grabbed his arm. "Come on, Pap." He bobbed his head toward the park. "Just come with me for a minute, in case I need you."

Owen resisted, leaning toward the church. Then, with a grunt of disgust, he surrendered. "All right, all right." He let Ethan help him down from the curb. "As long as we don't miss church, now that we've decided to go."

"Don't worry, we won't." Ethan looked both ways, then led Owen across the street. His heart was pounding like a drummer on a rampage in his chest; the secret plan was about to be realized.

Bright pink blossoms hung from the trees around them as they made their way around the corner and up the walk that cut diagonally through that part of the park. When they approached the bench where the little girl sat, they could hear her sobbing softly amid the tweets and chirps of the robins, sparrows, and wrens.

Ethan stopped a few feet away, holding Owen there with him, and cleared his throat. "Excuse me."

The girl, who couldn't have been older than six or seven, looked up at him. "Yes?" She wore a white sweater over a colorful Easter dress--knee-length, printed with tulips and lilies and daffodils.

"Are you all right?" asked Ethan. "We thought you might need help."

The little girl shook her head, then turned her gaze to Owen. "Mister?" A pair of bright pink clips held her hair back at the temples. "What's your name?"

Frowning, Owen hesitated. "Owen," he said finally.

"Owen." The girl nodded, then pushed herself off the bench to her feet. "Owen what?"

Again, Owen hesitated. "Talisman. Owen Talisman."

Smiling, the girl reached into the pocket of her little white sweater. "Then this is for you." She pulled out her hand, cupped her other hand over it, and reached up to Owen.

His frown really deepened at that. He leaned back, staring at her cupped hands as if they might contain a grenade.

Ethan put a reassuring arm around his shoulders. "Go ahead."

44

Owen shook his head. "But what if..."

"She's like six years old," said Ethan. "Go ahead, see what she's got for you."

Still, the old man hesitated.

"Please, Mister." The girl stepped closer and held her cupped hands higher. "It's an Easter present."

Owen scowled and tried to back away. "What kind of..."

Which was when he heard a sound from the little girl's hands. And his eyes shot wide open.

Then, he heard it again. It was a familiar sound, one he hadn't heard in ages but knew so well he could never forget it.

There it was again. A tiny, high-pitched chirp. Peep.

"Oh my God." Just as Owen said it, the girl opened her hands.

There between her little pink fingers was a fluffy yellow chick, a peep just like Blondie had once been.

"Here, Owen." She pressed it toward him.

Owen took the chick in his withered, shaking hands. He couldn't take his eyes off the baby bird as it chirped and squirmed in his grip.

Ethan, in turn, watched Owen's face closely. Was that a trace of a smile he saw on that wrinkled visage he loved so well?

It didn't matter, because the secret plan wasn't done yet.

After giving Owen a moment to take in the chick, Ethan nodded at the little girl, giving her the cue to deliver her next lines.

"Greetings from the Bunny Brotherhood." The girl pulled one side of her sweater back, revealing the silver badge that was pinned to her dress. The letters "BB" were printed on the badge in white paint.

"The Brotherhood?" said Ethan. "You mean like with the high sign and everything?" He was prompting the girl, who'd forgotten to give the salute.

Nodding, she raised her right hand, then wiggled the index and middle fingers in the rabbit-ears salute. "A friend sends his regards," she said.

"Friend?" Owen frowned. "What friend?"

Just then, a boy stepped out from behind a nearby tree. He had red hair and freckles and looked about eight or nine years old. He was wearing a white button-down shirt, dark slacks, and a red tie with a Bunny Brotherhood badge pinned to it where the tie tack should have been. "He said to give you this." The boy walked over and held out a fist, then turned it palm up and uncurled his fingers. "He said you would know who he was."

Again, Owen's eyes widened. In the palm of the boy's hand, there was a tuft of white fur.

With the chick in one hand, Owen took the tuft of fur

in the other. He stared at them both, speechless, as the boy and girl looked on.

The boy cleared his throat. "He said it's been a long time since you heard from him. He said you'll want to catch up on all the news you've missed from Bunnyburg."

"But here's the thing." Another child emerged from behind another tree--a girl, a little older than the others, with short brown hair and a pale green dress. She wore a Bunny Brotherhood badge on the strap of her white vinyl purse. "It's been a really long time since you last heard from him. So there's lots of news. Much more than one or two or even three of us can tell."

"That's why he sent more of us." The fifth child's voice--the squeaky voice of a very young boy--came from somewhere nearby, though he couldn't be seen yet. "That's why he sent lots more."

Someone let loose a loud whistle, then, and children poured out from behind every tree in Central Park. They came from behind the statue of Joseph Johns (founder of Johnstown) and the twin cannons on either side of it. They came from behind the statue of a Civil War soldier from the 54th Pennsylvania Infantry. They marched from around the Pasquerilla Fountain, the gazebo, the war monument, and the memorial to the victims of the 1977 Johnstown Flood.

And all of them were dressed in their Easter finest,

wearing Bunny Brotherhood badges.

There were dozens of them, all converging on Owen... all recruited from the actual Bunny Brotherhood fan club that supported his Bunnyburg books. Ethan had enlisted them for this special day, to remind Owen of what his work meant and that his life had meaning and could continue to do so. He could never take away Owen's pain for the loss of his wife and partner, but maybe he could take his mind off it for just a little while.

And maybe he could give him new purpose to boot.

"Every one of us has a story," said the still-unseen fifth child with the squeaky voice. "We bring them to catch you up on what you've missed. Could you help us bring them to the world in turn?"

As Owen gazed at the crowd of children surrounding him, he looked confused...perhaps overwhelmed. "I don't understand." He sounded flustered when he spoke. "Why do all this...for me?"

"To keep Bunnyburg alive," said the unseen child.

"But I can't," said Owen. "I don't...I don't have an artist anymore."

"Sure you do," said Ethan, and then he raised his voice for the crowd. "How many of you can draw?"

Every child in the park shot his or her hand in the air, fluttering their fingers in the Bunny Brotherhood high sign.

Owen sniffed. "This is too much." His lips quivered. "I don't deserve any of this."

"Sure you do." Ethan put his arm around his great-grandfather and squeezed his shoulders. "Just ask him."

With that, the unseen child finally made himself seen, stepping out from behind a nearby bush. He was a skinny kid with dark hair, and he wore a light brown suit and dark brown tie--a suit that resembled the one that Owen's mom had bought three days before Easter in 1935.

But the suit wasn't the most interesting thing about the kid. There was something else, something that caught everyone's eye, from the littlest child in the crowd to Owen Talisman himself.

The interesting thing was this: the kid was cradling a white-furred rabbit in his arms.

Ethan felt Owen relax against him. When he looked at Owen's face, he saw that for once, there wasn't a frown carved there.

As the kid carried the white rabbit forward, the crowd parted before him. Some of the children petted the bunny as it passed, and many of them giggled and whispered among themselves.

The kid stopped in front of Owen. "You already know each other, right?" The kid lifted the rabbit, turning its face toward Owen. "You remember him, don't you?" He put his ear near the rabbit's mouth, pretending to hear it talk. "That's right, he's Owen Talisman. And you." He looked up at Owen. "You remember him, right?" He held up the rabbit for Owen to take.

Owen cradled the rabbit in the crook of his right arm while holding the peeping chick in his left hand. "Of course I do." For the first time in so long that Ethan couldn't remember, an actual smile flowed across Owen's face. "How could I forget Flutter Cottontail?"

At which point, all the children clapped. And so did Ethan.

"Can we tell you our stories now?" asked the little blonde girl from the bench. "Please?"

That was when Owen did something that made the whole secret plan worthwhile for Ethan, aka Chip, aka his great-grandson. He turned and gave him a wink, and there was a spark in his eye when he did it.

Then, Owen turned back to the kids. "Okay, one at a time," he said. "And somebody get me a pen and a notebook, so I can write everything down."

As soon as the words left his lips, the children of the Bunny Brotherhood swarmed around him, all telling their stories at once, all tugging his sleeves, all reaching for Flutter Cottontail, the once and future king of the kingdom of Bunnyburg.

ABOUT THE AUTHOR

Robert Jeschonek is an award-winning writer whose fiction, comics, essays, articles, and podcasts have been published around the world. DC Comics, Simon & Schuster, and DAW have published his work. His young adult slipstream fantasy novel, *My Favorite Band Does Not Exist*, won the Forward National Literature Award and was named a Top Ten First Novel for Youth by *Booklist*. His cross-genre science fiction thriller, *Day 9*, is an International Book Award winner. He also won the Scribe Award for Best Original Novel from the International Association of Media Tie-in Writers for his alternate history, *Tannhäuser: Rising Sun, Falling Shadows*. He was nominated for the British Fantasy Award for his story, "Fear of Rain." Visit him online at www.robertjeschonek.com. You can also find him on Facebook and follow him as @TheFictioneer on Twitter.

ANOTHER GREAT JOHNSTOWN STORY NOW AVAILABLE FROM ROBERT JESCHONEK

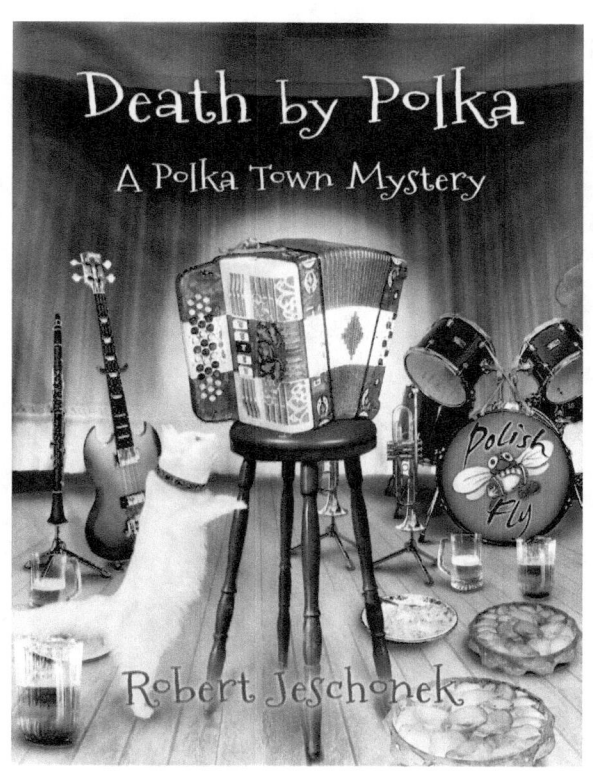

DEATH BY POLKA

BY ROBERT JESCHONEK

Who killed Polish Lou, the famous Prince of Polka Music? His daughter, musicologist Lottie Kachowski, comes home to the polka heartland of Johnstown, Pennsylvania, to find the answer. Lottie has an unbeatable talent for using music to solve crimes, and she does just that on the trail of her father's killer. But the stakes turn deadlier than ever when another polka legend comes to a tragic end. As the danger rises, Lottie recruits her father's wacky girlfriend, Polish Peg, to help her dig deeper into the wild world of small town polka. At the same time, she fights to keep from getting dragged back into the polka scene she left behind long ago.

AND NOW, A SPECIAL PREVIEW OF DEATH BY POLKA...

As I looked out over the crowd in the banquet hall, the Furies glared back at me in disgust. There were three of them, all dressed in black, all with raven black hair, and they were my sisters.

Bonnie, the oldest and tallest, stood in the middle. Her brown eyes framed a big, angular nose that gave her the look of a hawk. Her hair was long, draped over her shoulders, but not nearly as long as mine.

Charlie stood at her side. She was shorter and rounder than any of us, with plump cheeks and dark blue eyes. Her hair was cut in a kind of dowdy helmet 'do that made her look older than she was, older than any of us.

Then there was Ellie, the youngest. She looked like an anorexic teen, all skin and bones and giant blue eyes so pale they were almost white. Those eyes peering out from

1

her shag haircut with the spiky bangs looked perpetually challenging, always ready to go off.

Which, actually, described her personality. All *three* of the Furies' personalities.

Boy did they have capital "T" tempers. They were always, *always* fighting with each other, shifting alliances, holding grudges on top of grudges.

But today, for once, they were united against a common object of resentment. *Me*, in other words. I had the honor of having brought them together in harmony. I could see it in their body language as they all clustered together and stared up at me through slitted eyes. I could feel it in the air, and I could guess what had brought it on.

They were mad that I was the only sister called up on stage. It didn't matter that I didn't *want* to be there; I knew my sisters, and I *knew* this was eating them alive.

It was just the latest in a series of injustices. First, I'd gone off to Los Angeles while they'd all stayed in town and given birth to the ADHD Dozen. Then, I'd gotten engaged, while the best they'd been able to manage was a string of deadbeat baby daddies. Now this.

I knew I'd pay for it later, but I chose to ignore them for now. Basil Sloveski was waving a number ten white business envelope over his giant silver pompadour.

"All right, folks!" The corners of Basil's eyes crinkled as

he grinned. Up close, I could see his whole overtanned face was a web of fine lines. "Without further ado!"

The crowd roared (except for the Furies, who just rolled their eyes) and pumped beers in the air. The ADHD Dozen squirmed their way up front and lined up along the stage, screeching and dancing like idiots.

"How about a drum roll, guys?" When Basil said it, Eddie Sr.'s ancient drummer hopped up on the stage, raised his bony arms in a weight-lifter's pose with fists curled toward his shaggy white head, and dropped down on the squeaky red stool behind his drum kit.

As the drum roll started, Basil slid a fingernail under the corner of the envelope flap, then dragged his nail along the length of the flap, tearing it open with a ripping sound.

My heart pounded, and I held my breath. As badly as I didn't want to be there, I was actually caught up in the suspense. Polish Lou's showmanship had broken through even my tough exterior.

The kids down in front couldn't stand the suspense either. They were hopping up and down, clawing at the stage, having conniptions. Milly spoke for all of them. "*What? What's it say?*"

Basil slipped two tanned fingers into the envelope and drew out a folded sheet of paper. He cleared his throat as he unfolded it, playing up the drama.

3

Then, he started reading. "Dear fellow polka lovers!" The drum roll continued in the background as Basil's voice rang over the crowd. "As you know, I've been called the Prince of Pennsylvania Polka."

The crowd roared its approval.

"But now that the *Prince* is dead, who will rule his *kingdom?*" Basil paused and looked around the banquet hall for dramatic effect. "Who will be my *successor?*"

"*Who? Who?*" squeaked one of the kids down in front.

"Who will carry on the tradition of great polka music as leader of my band, Polish Fly?" read Basil. "Who will continue to broadcast three hours of polkatacular tunetasticness every Saturday morning and Sunday afternoon on my radio show, *Kocham Taniec?*

"Who will organize the annual Polkapourri festival that has become an institution for Johnstown and the entire tri-state area?

"And who will manage Polish Lou Enterprises now that Polish Lou is gone?" Basil stopped reading aloud, though his eyes kept scanning the page. He got a funny look on his face, a kind of smirking frown, like he wasn't sure he'd read the letter correctly. Then he shrugged, nodded, and gazed out at the crowd. "I'll tell you who!

"*She* will!" With that, Basil swung an arm around and pointed directly at Peg.

4

The drum roll ended with a rim shot, and the crowd cheered like crazy. Eddie Sr. and Eddie Jr. played wild strains on their accordions. In front of the stage, the kids spun and jumped and gyrated like human popcorn in their little suits and dresses.

Glancing at the Furies, I saw the three of them looked more thoroughly disgusted than ever. One thing they all had in common and shared with me was an undying hatred of Polish Peg.

As for the Clown herself, she beamed and waved with pure delight. If I hadn't known any better, I might've thought she'd just won the Miss America pageant or an Academy Award.

Clapping politely, I turned away and looked for the best place to step down from the stage. The crowd was slightly thinner by the corner, so maybe that would be a good exit point.

Just as I took a step toward the corner, Basil called out behind me. "And *she* will, too!"

I swear, everyone in the banquet hall gasped at once. Except me.

"That's right!" said Basil. "I'm talking about *you*, Lottie!"

At the mention of my name, I spun to face him. "Me, what?"

"You're the *co-queen* of Lou's kingdom, that's what!"

5

Basil lunged over and grabbed my arm, then hauled it high like I'd just won a prize fight. "Ladies and polkamen! Meet the new rulers of Polka Land! Lou's own daughter, Lottie..." Basil grabbed Peg's arm and hefted it overhead alongside mine. "...and his partner, the love of his life, Polish Peg!"

The crowd went berserk. Cameras flashed in my eyes as Eddie Sr. and Eddie Jr. launched into "Hail to the Chief" on their accordions.

Dazed, I leaned forward and looked past Basil at Peg. The look on her clownish face said it all.

She was as surprised as I was. And just about as happy.

Which, let me tell you, wasn't happy at all.

ALSO BY ROBERT JESCHONEK

LONG LIVE GLOSSER'S
(A History of the Glosser Bros. Department Store)

CHRISTMAS AT GLOSSER'S

FEAR OF RAIN
(A Johnstown Flood Story)

THE MASKED FAMILY
(A Cambria County Story)

NOW ON SALE AT AMAZON.COM, BARNESANDNOBLE.COM, OR BY REQUEST AT YOUR LOCAL BOOKSTORE

Ask your bookseller to search by title at Amazon, Ingram, or Baker and Taylor.

"Robert Jeschonek is a towering talent." – Mike Resnick, Hugo and Nebula Award-winning author of the *Starship* series

"Robert Jeschonek is the literary love child of Tim Burton and Neil Gaiman. His fiction is cutting edge, original, and pulsing with dark and fantastical life." – Adrian Phoenix, critically acclaimed author of *The Maker's Song* and *Hoodoo* series

Pie Press